一線入魂
石井義人
作　品　集
Line into the soul
Yoshito ISHII  Works

一線入魂　　　　Line into the soul

石井義人 作品集　　Yoshito ISHII Works

製作人　　Uspace Gallery
作者　　　楊青芬
藝術家　　石井 義人　Yoshito ISHII
編輯出版　宇達特文創有限公司
　　　　　台北市大安區敦化南路一段312號 (02)2700-6883
E-mail　　service@urdct.com
視覺設計　宇威數位設計股份有限公司 (02)2705-6308
發行　　　時報文化出版企業股份有限公司
　　　　　桃園縣龜山鄉萬壽路二段351號 (02)2306-6842

初版一刷　2018年8月
定價　　　新台幣900 元

ISBN　　　978-986-90070-3-0

# 目錄 Contents

# 院體派的精細 文人畫的風骨

至攄發胸意，則於高堂素壁，放手作長松巨木，回溪斷岩，
岩岫巉絕，峰巒秀起，雲煙變滅，掩靄之間，千態萬狀。

"宣和畫譜(西元1120年),論郭熙"

石井義人應是我接觸過最孤僻的藝術家；在為他設辦的歡聚場合，
他永遠看來像走錯門而窘促尷尬的孩子，話不多，也不會低頭滑手
機（因為他堅持手機只拿來通話）；但觀看他的作品，會驚訝他腦
海裡的小宇宙如此複雜又縝密，以絲絲曲線結合美麗的圖騰，勾勒
出氣勢磅礡的胸壑，殷勤訴說他創作的熱情。

石井的作品細密而繁複，以髮絲猶不及的針筆，取自大地的簡樸墨
色，烟藍、石榴紅等，描摹著如山坡野林的千變景緻。
顆顆的種子，在如雪般的白紙上慢慢萌芽，茁壯。其或是山野中飄
逸的芒草、澤畔的小花；或是竹林裡紛飛的鳥羽、秋荷上的一滴露。
石井的畫，就如自然的幻化，難以一眼窺透。

「抽象圖形對我來說就像種子一樣。我想做個農夫，灌溉這些種子，
直到有一天它們茁壯成長」——石井義人。

長年的藝術學習薰陶，不論西畫或水墨，他擁一身訓練有素的好技
能；但是創作者總想走出原創的一條路，沉澱數年後他發想出了絕
無僅有的抽象針筆畫！以日本傳統紋樣為種子，從中國兩宋畫派精
神為師，石井的畫細緻纏綿，完全無法被傳統藝評框架，也因為其
流暢優雅線條成為特色，罕少能出其右！

宋朝是中國繪畫史上的黃金時代，院體畫和文人畫兩脈爭鋒，院體
畫這類作品為迎合帝王宮廷需要，多以花鳥、山水、宮廷生活及宗
教內容為題材，作畫講究法度，重視形神兼備，風格華麗細膩。
而文人畫則強調氣韻，多為抒發性靈之作，注重意境的闡釋。

書畫雙絕的藝術家皇帝徽宗,把宋朝的畫院帶入了一個嶄新的境界;徽宗開設「畫學」,所有應募者都必須根據太學法加以考試,目的主要在看這些畫工的繪畫技巧,是否合乎其有藝術修養的文人與士大夫的鑑賞標準;箇中翹楚即是郭熙,郭熙所完成的風格平遠形式,以及使畫面具有深遠感的意欲。(見附圖 早春圖/青盛)

此圖為郭熙傳世名作,通過山間霧靄浮動及旭陽照射的氣候描繪,細緻而生動地畫出嚴冬剛剛過去,春天悄然降臨的微妙變化,從中傳達出歡慰喜悅的感情。

和郭熙作品相較,石井義人的畫作氣韻神似,成功地將工筆畫的技巧、細膩,同文人畫深遠的意蘊完美的融合。

文人氣息甚有過之的是,石井義人將畫作以主觀選出無意涵的古漢字——命名,秉著近乎偏執的意念,透過古名的讀音和細膩的筆觸兜轉,石井義人詮釋的是時間傳遞的雅致品味。

早春圖(現存台灣故宮博物院)
質地:絹本
幅面:縱15.83*10.8 cm

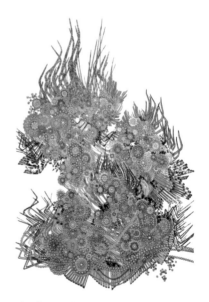

青盛 ( Sei Sei )
ink on Kent paper
116.7*80.3 cm

# 石井 義人

1980年
群馬県伊勢崎市生まれ

2003年
日本大学芸術学部
美術学科絵画コース版画専攻卒業

## 個展

２００９　イシイヨシト「阿吽A」SAKuRA GALLERY　東京
２０１１　イシイヨシト・ペン画展「ani-millimism」FUMA CONTEMPORARY
２０１４　イシイヨシト・ペン画展「線乃ざわめき。」The Art complex
　　　　Center of Tokyo
２０１５　イシイヨシト・ペン画展「続・線乃ざわめき。」ギャルリー志門 東京
２０１６　渺渺 - 極線之美　Uspace Gallery　台北
２０１７　一線入魂　Uspace Gallery　台北

## グループ展

１９９９　群馬青年ビエンナーレ'99　群馬県立近代美術館
２０００　デザインフェスタvol.11 東京ビッグサイト　東京
２００２　第２６回全国大学版画展　国際版画美術館　東京
２００３　東京五美術大学連合卒業・修了制作展　東京都美術館
２０１０　N＋N展2010春の嵐:日藝美術出身の若手作家達の今 練馬区立美術館
　　　　meet展　SAKuRA GALLERY　東京
　　　　第26回FUKUIサムホール美術展
２０１１　ACTアート大賞展　The Art complex Center of Tokyo
　　　　N＋N 展2011　生命を見つめる　練馬区立美術館　東京
　　　　あおぞらDEアート8人展　SAKuRA gallery　東京
　　　　細密展3　The Art complex Center of Tokyo
２０１２　細密展4　The Art complex Center of Tokyo
　　　　第17回アートムーブ絵画コンクール展 大阪市立生涯学習センターギャラリー
　　　　第29回FUKUIサムホール美術展
　　　　大細密展　The Art complex Center of Tokyo
２０１３　Sensai展　The Art complex Center of Tokyo
　　　　常設展　gallery art soup　群馬
　　　　裏カーボンブラック　SELF-SO gallery　京都
２０１４　ACT小品展2014　The Art complex Center of Tokyo
　　　　C/LABORATORY PROJECT@ Hong Kong Contemporary 2014
　　　　第31回FUKUIサムホール美術展
　　　　ACT+ISM　The Art complex Center of Tokyo
　　　　アートの贈り物 -眠れない夜に-　銀座三越　東京

２０１５　清須市第８回はるひ絵画トリエンナーレ
２０１６　語る抽象画展　The Art complex Center of Tokyo
Infinity Japan 2016 Contemporary Art Show in Taipei
小名木川バラッド　SAKuRA Gallery　東京
第33回FUKUIサムホール美術展
神戸アートマルシェ2016
第26回FUKUIサムホール美術展
METRO ART vol.25 @東京サンケイビル秋まつり
２０１７　METRO ART vol.26 東京サンケイビル　東京
Infinity Japan 2017 Contemporary Art Show in Taipei
細密展11　The Art complex Center of Tokyo
アートスープ．クロニクル　gallery art soup　群馬
Cross the River　SAKuRA Gallery　東京
大細密展2017　The Art complex Center of Tokyo　東京
水無月-日本當代藝術特展　Uspace Gallery　台北 台湾
第34回FUKUIサムホール美術展
アートフェアアジア福岡　ホテルオークラ福岡
神戸アートマルシェ2017
高秋山景　SAKuRA Gallery　東京
ペン画三人展　創世の細部　ギャラリーボイス　岩手
２０１８　Infinity Japan 2018・プレエキシビション　Uspace Gallery
細密展12 - 緻 -　The Art complex Center of Tokyo
Infinity Japan 2018 Contemporary Art Show in Taipei
Artsoup in Colmena vol.2　Colmena Gallery & Art Space
アートフェア東京2018　東京国際フォーラム
石川画廊　東京
EXTRA ART 2　The Art complex Center of Tokyo

**受賞歴**

１９９９　群馬青年ビエンナーレ'99　入選
２０１０　第26回FUKUIサムホール美術展　入選
第6回全国公募西脇市サムホール美術展　入選
２０１２　第17回アートムーブ絵画コンクール　ドリーム賞
第29回FUKUIサムホール美術展　入選
第7回西脇市サムホール美術展　入選
２０１４　大細密展　優秀賞
第9回全国公募西脇市サムホール美術展　入選
第31回FUKUIサムホール美術展　奨励賞
２０１５　第8回清須絵画トリエンナーレ　佳作
２０１６　第33回FUKUIサムホール美術展　入選
２０１７　第34回FUKUIサムホール美術展　入選

# Yoshito ISHII

1 9 8 0　Born in Isesaki City,Gunma,Japan ,Living in Takasaki City,Gunma,Japan
2 0 0 2　Graduated from Nihon University College Of Art,
　　　　　The Department Of Fine Arts

## Solo Exhibitions

2 0 0 9　A-Un(阿吽),at Sakura Gallery,Tokyo,Japan
2 0 1 1　Ani-Millimism, at FUMA CONTEMPORARY Tokyo
2 0 1 4　Sen no Zawameki(線乃ざわめき), at The Art Complex Center of Tokyo
2 0 1 5　Zoku Sen no Zawameki(続・線乃ざわめき), at Gallery Shimon
2 0 1 6　ByoByo -Kyokusen no bi-(渺渺 - 極線の美 - )at Uspace gallery,Taipei
2 0 1 7　Issen Nyukon(一線入魂), at Uspace gallery,Taipei
2 0 1 8　繾綣 Lingering , at Uspace gallery,Taipei

## Group Exhibitions

1 9 9 9　Gunma Biennale for Young Artists 99'
2 0 0 0　Design Festa Vol.11,at Tokyo Big Sight
2 0 0 2　The 26th Annual Exhibition of The Association of Japanese Art Colleges,
　　　　　at Machida City Museum of Graphic Arts
2 0 0 3　Joint Graduation Exhibition of Five Art Universities in Tokyo
2 0 1 0　Exhibition N + N 2010 The First Spring Storm in Nerima :Art Now of
　　　　　the Young Graduates of Nichigei Fine Arts, at Nerima Art Museum
　　　　　Meets, at Sakura Gallery,Tokyo,Japan
　　　　　The 26th Fukui Thumb Hole Art Exhibition, at Fukui Culture Center
2 0 1 1　ACT Art Award, at The Art Complex Center of Tokyo
　　　　　The 3rd Saimitsu Exhibition 2011,at The Art Complex Center of Tokyo
　　　　　Exhibition N＋N 2011 Gazing at the Life: Works of Art of the Teaching
　　　　　Staffs and Graduates of Nichigei Fine Arts, at Nerima Art Museum
　　　　　Aozora De Art Exhibition, at Sakura Gallery,Tokyo,Japan
　　　　　The 4th Saimitsu Exhibition, at The Art Complex Center of Tokyo
2 0 1 2　The 17th Art Move Award, at Osaka,Japan
　　　　　DaiSaimitsu Exhibition, at The Art Complex Center of Tokyo
　　　　　The 29th Fukui Thumbhole Art Exhibition, at Fukui Culture Center
2 0 1 3　Permanent Exhibition, at Gallery Art Soup,Gunma,Japan
　　　　　Ura Carbon Black,SELF-SO gallery,Kyoto,Japan
2 0 1 4　Shohin Exhibition2014,at The Art Complex Center of Tokyo
　　　　　C/LABORATORY PROJECT@ HONG KONG CONTEMPORARY 2014
　　　　　The 31th Fukui Thumbhole Art Exhibition, at Fukui Culture Center
　　　　　ACT+ISM, at The Art complex Center of Tokyo
　　　　　Gift Of Art -For Sleepless Night- at Ginza Mitsukoshi,Tokyo,Japan

２０１５  The 8th Kiyosu City Haruhi Painting Triennale,at Kiyosu Haruhi
        Museum,Kiyosu City Library,Aichi,Japan
２０１６  Talking Abstract Paintings Exhibition, at The Art Complex Center of Tokyo
        Infinity Japan 2016 Contemporary Art Show, at MIRAMAR GARDEN TAIPEI
        Onagigawa Ballad,at SAKuRA Gallery,Tokyo,Japan
        The 33th Fukui Thumbhole Art Exhibition, at Fukui Culture Cente
        Kobe Art Marche,at Kobe Meriken Park Hotel
        METRO ART vol.25 @Tokyo Sankei building Autumn Festival
２０１７  METRO ART vol.26,at Tokyo Sankei building
        Infinity Japan 2017 Contemporary Art Show,at MIRAMAR GARDEN TAIPEI
        Saimitsu Exhibition 11,at The Art Complex Center of Tokyo
        Art Soup chronicle,at Gallery Art Soup,Gunma,Japan
        Cross the River,at SAKuRA Gallery
        DaiSaimitsu Exhibition 2017,at The Art Complex Center of Tokyo
        Minaduki-Japanese Contemporary Art Special Exhibition
        ,at Uspace gallery,Taipei,Taiwan

        The 34th Fukui Thumbhole Art Exhibition,at Fukui Culture Center
        Art Fair Asia Fukuoka,at Hotel Okura Fukuoka
        Kobe Art Marche 2017,at Kobe Meriken Park Hotel
２０１８  Kosyu sankei,at SAKuRA Gallery,Tokyo,Japan
        Detail of Genesis,at Gallery Voice,Iwate,Japan
        Infinity Japan 2018 Pre-Exhibition,at Uspace Gallery,Taipei
        Saimitsu Exhibition 12,at The Art Complex Center of Tokyo
        Infinity Japan 2018 Contemporary Art Show,at Hotel Royal Nikko Taipei
        Artsoup in Colmena vol.2,at Colmena Gallery & Art Space
        ART FAIR TOKYO 2018,at Tokyo International Forum,Tokyo
        Permanent Exhibition(during ART FAIR TOKYO2018 ),at IshikawaGallery
        EXTRA ART 2,at The Art complex Center of Tokyo

## Awards
１９９９  Selected for Biennale of Young Artist Gunma
２０１０  Selected for The 27th Competition of Fukui Thumbhole Size Painting
        Selected for The 8th Competition of Nishiwaki Thumbhole Size Painting
２０１２  Selected for The 9th Competition of Nishiwaki Thumbhole Size Painting
        Selected for The 29th Competition of Fukui Thumbhole Size Painting
        Dream Award for The 17th Art Move Award
        Award of Excellence for DaiSaimitsu Exhibition
２０１４  Encouragement Award for The 31th Competition of Fukui
        Thumbhole  Size Painting
２０１５  A fine work for The 8th Kiyosu City Painting triennale
２０１６  Selected for The 33th Competition of Fukui Thumbhole Size Painting
２０１７  Selected for The 34th Competition of Fukui Thumbhole Size Painting

# コンセプトのようなもの
イシイヨシト

「この作品は何を描いたものですか」とオーディエンスから質問を受けることがよくあります。
私は学生時代、「人間の顔」をテーマにしていました。当時の私は顔の造形に惹かれていて、STAEDTLERの一番濃い鉛筆で半ば偏執的に何枚も描いていました。衝動的に描いたものが多く、作品として結実したものは多くありません。やがて大学卒業が近づくに連れ、制作に悩むようになりました。顔というモチーフをこの先作品としてどう広げていけばよいかわからなくなり、制作に対して心が強張り、考え過ぎて作品が作れない状況が卒業後しばらく続きました。

ある時、顔の凹凸を長い線で丁寧に追いながら描いてみました。
ミニマリスティックに並んだ線の様子がなんとなく心地良いものに感じられました。顔という具体的なモチーフが消え、線はやがて曲線となり、模様へと変化していきました。模様はやがて重なり合い、
徐々に今の作風へ近づいていきました。そんな風に作風を確立していった時期が二十代全般です。

経歴にもありますが、その頃は殆ど作品の発表をしていません。
学生時代からの頑なな考えからまだ抜け出せず「自分の作品はまだ人前に出すほどのものではない」と考えていたからです。
心の強張りを解きほぐすように、作品も形態がより自由になり色彩が加わり、世界が広がっていったように思います。
例えば日本の茶道における茶碗の世界では、ひとつひとつの茶碗を個別の作品として観るよりも一人の作家が焼いた複数の茶碗を系統的に眺めることで初めてその作家性や良さが浮かび上がる、という事があります。

私が作品を作る際にも一点一点に個別のコンセプトを設定して作っているわけではありません。あくまでも呼吸するように描き、その呼吸のひと区切り・吹き溜まりとして形を為したものが作品である、という認識を持っています。

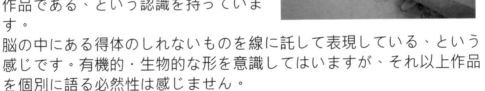

脳の中にある得体のしれないものを線に託して表現している、という感じです。有機的・生物的な形を意識してはいますが、それ以上作品を個別に語る必然性は感じません。

## 作品のタイトルと読み方について

タイトルは作品が完成した後、「漢典」( http://www.zdic.net/ ) などの
サイトで検索して漢字を選んで決めます。その字について何度も検索
し、意味を調べ特に悪い意味でなければ採用します。
青を基調にした作品では「青」の部首が付く漢字、赤を基調にした作
品なら「赤」や「紅」の入ったタイトル、という風にその都度作品に
合わせて決めていきます。
かといって特に法則性があるわけではなく、あくまでも便宜上つけた
名前、という風に理解して頂ければと思います。読み方も日本語の読
み方や中国語の読み方、あるいは万葉仮名 ( 古代日本で漢字が普及し始めた時
に、日本語の読み方に合わせて音の近い漢字を当てたもの ) 風のタイトルにするな
ど、その都度作品のイメージ ( 私の作品の場合、専ら色彩と形態からのイメージだ
けですが ) に合わせて工夫します。

## タイトルに漢字を使用する理由について

膨大な文字数を誇る漢字は、一文字一文字の意味が非常に深淵且つ多
岐に渡り、完全に理解する事など専門家でも不可能な表意文字です。
殊に我々日本人にとって漢字は日常的に親しんでいる文字である反
面、理解不能な呪術性の強い文字でもあります。
前述の通り、私は作品内で何か具体的なモチーフを描いているわけで
はなく、また文章にできるような明確なコンセプトに基づいて描いて
いるわけではありません。
本来は「無題」でもよいのですが、言葉で説明しようのない作品には
難解な文字がふさわしかろうと思い、普段日本人が使わないような漢
字を選んで採用しています。 ( PCによっては表示されない場合もあります
ので便宜上アルファベットで読み方もつけてありますが、本来ならば作品タイトルは極力漢
字で、アルファベット抜きで表示してほしいというのが本音です。作家としてはオーディエ
ンスがタイトルの読み方や意味を理解する必要などなく、寧ろ作品とタイトルの組み合わせ
からくる違和感を楽しんでほしい、という事です。 )

例えば故宮博物院で商代や周代の素晴らしい青銅器群に接する際、
誰がキャプションに書かれているあの難解な漢字の本当の意味を理解
できるでしょう。しかもそのタイトルは作者が名付けたものではな
く、後世の研究者がそれぞれの青銅器の用途を形態から推測し、
それにふさわしい名前を付けたに過ぎません。

ですが我々はキャプションに記載されている難解な漢字の持つ呪術性
も含めて、あの時代の人々の不可思議な造形感覚に触れる事が出来る
わけで、私の作品と作品タイトルもまた同様に観ていただければ、と
思っているのです。

**「這件作品在畫什麼樣的東西呢？」**經常會從觀看者那邊聽到這樣的疑問。
在學生時代我以「人臉」作為創作主題，當時的我被臉的造型深深吸引，
使用STAEDTLER素描筆中色號最濃的鉛筆，近乎偏執的狀態畫了無數的作品。
因為一時衝動而畫下的多半是練習作，能夠稱為作品的為數不多。大學畢業的
前夕，我開始思索關於創作這件事情。
我不知道以臉為主題的作品該如何提升廣度，對於創作這件事情十分煩惱、
因為思慮太多導致無法創作的狀況在畢業後仍然持續著。有時候，我試著用很
長的線並且仔細的描繪不一致的臉型。不知不覺對於簡潔線條整齊排列的樣子
感到愉悅。抽離以具象的臉為主題的方向後，線條轉變為以曲線的方式表現圖
紋。各種圖紋開始重疊，漸漸的轉變為現在的風格，這樣的創作風格大概在二
十歲左右確立。那個時候也經歷了求職，而在這個時期基本上沒有發表任何作
品，會這麼做是因為從學生時代起便一直認為「自己的作品還沒有到能夠拿出
來給人們看的程度」。
確立風格後，心中糾結的點像是解開一樣，作品的樣貌能夠變得更加自由並增
添色彩、世界觀也變得更加廣闊。像是日本的茶道中的茶碗，比起將茶碗作為
個別的作品來看待，從一位藝術家所燒製出來的總體作品來欣賞更能看出這位
藝術家的精湛技巧。而我的作品在創作時也並非是都擁有不同的概念的個別作
品，而是能夠意識到像是在描繪著呼吸，當時的換氣、吹氣各種狀態化為形體
的創作，將心中那些不盡分明的想法寄託於線條表現出來。這樣能夠將作品視
為有機體、生物的型態，但是不需要更多的言語去闡述。

## 作品標題的唸法

標題是在作品完成後，於「漢典」（ http://www.zdic.net/ ）之類的網站上搜尋的漢
字決定的。每個字都會不停地搜尋、確認沒有特別不好的意思後再決定使用。
以青色為基調的作品便以部首「青」這個漢字為主題；若是紅色基調的作品便以
「赤」或是「紅」兩個漢字為題目並且根據作品的風格再決定使用什麼樣的漢字
做組合。換句話說，標題只是單純以較為方便的方式命名，並非有什麼特別的規
範來決定。唸法的部分，無論是日文的讀音、中文的讀音，又或是萬葉假名（古
代的日本在漢字普及前，日文的發音和漢字本身發音很相近）作為標題使用之類的，都會隨
著每一件作品的圖像（單指圖像各別的色彩、造型等）再做調整。

## 為何標題使用漢字？

博大精深的漢字，個別都擁有著深厚的意思，要完全理解每個漢字字面上的意思
的話，不是專家無法辦得到；特別是對於日本人來說也會遇到漢字像是咒語一般
不能理解的狀況。
像前面所說的，我的作品並沒有具體主題、或是能夠像撰寫文章一般有明確的概念
作為基底、進而描繪出來的狀況。本來取名為「無題」也是可以的，但我想無法輕
易用言語解釋的創作，這樣一來使用很難理解的文字也很合適，因此選擇了平常日
本人不會使用到的古漢字。（在電腦上也有無法顯示的情況，為了讀音方便會加註拼音，事實
上標題的部分是非常希望將拼音拿掉，單純使用漢字表現。以創作者的角度來說，比起觀者希望理解
標題的唸法、字面上的意義，我更加希望他們能夠將作品和標題組合後享受兩者不對稱的樂趣。）

例如在故宮博物院裡，接觸到的那些商朝或是周朝精美的青銅器，不知道是誰取的品名，但是那些看起來深奧的漢字卻又能被輕易理解。那些標題並非是由作者特別取名的，而是後世的研究者們透過個別青銅器的用途、形態等推測後，給他們各自取了適合的名字。但是，在這些我們看起來深奧難以理解的漢字，在當時是因為那個時代，人們當下接觸了各種對於造型感受到的不可思議的經驗而被創造出來的，我也希望我的作品及標題，在被觀看時也能夠讓觀者如此體會。

## I often get this question from the audience: What is this drawing about?

I was devoted to 'Human Faces' when I was a student. I was very captivated by the shapes of faces back then and would use the darkest STAEDTLER pencil and draw many, many pieces of it in a semi monomaniacal manner. A lot of those were impulse drawings and most of them could not be deemed as completed art works.
Before long, I started to worry over production as my university graduation approached. I got more and more unsure as to how my work based on face motifs would unfold, my heart got knotted up over production, and I eventually could not produce any work from overthinking it, even for a good while after I graduated.

I once tried to carefully trace and draw the unevenness of a face in one long line. This minimalistic-like line drawing felt pleasant to me for some reason or another. The specific motif of the face had disappeared, the lines morphed into curves and transformed into a pattern. These patterns soon overlapped each other and gradually became my current art style. I spent the whole of my twenties fine-tuning and establishing my art style this way. Throughout that entire period I almost never published any work except for a few. The reason was because I could not break out from my obstinate ideas ever since my undergraduate days and thought that my works back then were not something that I could show anyone at all.
As the tension and apprehension in my heart started to unravel and melt away, my works also started to take on a freer and more colorful form than before. I then began to think that my world was going to unfold before my eyes.For example, in the world of teacups in the Japanese art of tea ceremony, rather than looking at these teacups as individual works of art, one gets a better sense of the artist's character and ingenuity from a set of tea cups baked by the artist, even if it is the first time the person is viewing it. This is also the same for me; I do not aim to set individual concepts separately as I create my works. My approach to drawing is absolutely akin to how I breathe. I draw with the notion that I want to capture and materialize every interval and cumulation of my breathing into art works. It is like an expression of the nondescript things in my head in lines. While I am conscious of these organic and biological shapes and forms, I do not see the necessity in expressing each and individual work separately beyond this.

## How to read the titles of the works.

After the works are completed, I will search via online Chinese dictionary websites such as '漢典' (www.zdic.net) and then choose and decide the Chinese characters I want. I will only use that character after running it through multiple checks and making sure that it does not mean anything bad or evil.

Titles for works based on the color blue will have characters containing the 'blue' (青) radical, and similarly, characters containing radicals such as 赤 and 紅 ('red') will be used for works drawn in red. This is how I tailor and decide the titles for my works each time. But having said that I actually do not have any particular rule in mind; these characters and titles aremerely chosen out of convenience and simplicity.I also try to be creative with the titles by choosing those that complement the image of the works (solely based on the images of colors and forms in my case though). The titles are especially chosen in different styles where they are either read in Japanese pronunciation, Chinese pronunciation, or Man'yōgana style (an ancient writing system that employs Chinese characters to represent the Japanese language and was the first known kana system to be developed as a means to represent the Japanese language phonetically).

**Reasons on why Chinese characters are used in titles.**

The Chinese character system boasts of thousands and thousands of different characters where their meanings are extremely deep and cover a wide range of topics. It is impossible even for experts to fully understand each and every Chinese character. Even though we Japanese use these characters every day and are familiar with them, on the other hand, there are also many magic-imbued characters that we simply cannot understand. As previously mentioned, there are no particular motifs in my works and I do not draw with a clear concept in my mind that can be easily expressed into words too. I suppose 'Untitled' would be a good title for my works but I started to think that perhaps I should use obscure words to describe these works that cannot be explained instead.

This is why I ended up choosing words that Japanese do not usually use or encounter. (Since these characters occasionally cannot be even displayed depending on the computer, I have also attached the alphabetical pronunciation out of convenience for the viewer. However, these titles are entirely made up of Chinese characters and if possible, I actually wanted them to appear as they are without the alphabetical pronunciation.

As an artist, I do not think it is necessary for the audience to be able to read the titles or understand its meaning. In fact, I would very much prefer if they could enjoy the discomfort arising from the combination of the work and the titles instead.)

For example, I do not think any one actually understands the real meaning behind the obscure characters used in the captions for the magnificent bronzeware from the Shang Dynasty or Zhou Dynasty when they see them in the Palace Museum in Taiwan.

Not to mention that those titles were actually not given by the artists or creators, but by researchers in later times who had to deduce the purposes of the bronzeware from their shapes and consequently give appropr-iate names. Nevertheless, through the obsc-ure and hard-to-understand, incantation-like characters used in the captions, we are able to experience and get a sense of the amazing creation skills of the people of that era. I would also very much hope for the same for my works and their titles too.

見形是形

2003
|
2005

厌 (Zha)

graphite on watercolor paper
15.8x22.7(cm)

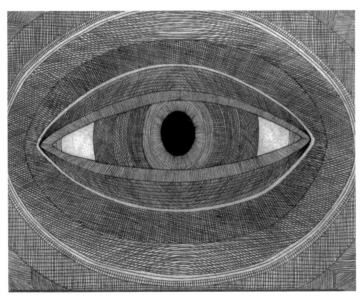

阿 (A)

graphite on watercolor paper
15.8x22.7(cm)

眼之一

graphite on watercolor paper
53x45.5(cm)

眼之二

graphite on watercolor paper
53x53(cm)

眼之三

graphite on watercolor paper
53x53.1(cm)

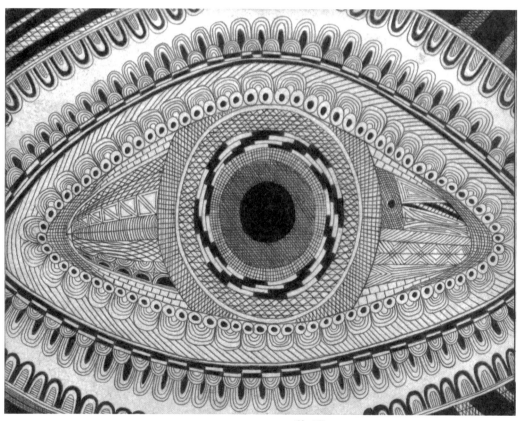

妝眼 (Shoyan)
graphite on watercolor paper
15.8x22.7(cm)

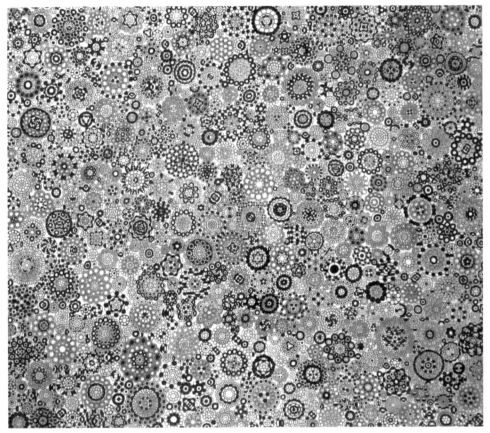

茫 (Bou)
graphite on watercolor paper

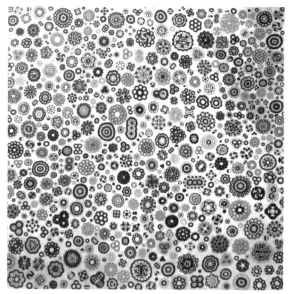

斑眼 (Madarame)

graphite on watercolor paper
53x53(cm)

胎華 (TaiKa)

graphite on watercolor paper
41x31.8(cm)

**叕叕** (Tetsutetsu)

graphite on watercolor paper
72.7x72.7(cm)

**渾渾** (KonKon)

graphite on watercolor paper
38x45.5(cm)

**蠢蠢** (ShunShun)

graphite on watercolor paper
41x31.8(cm)

**小曄** (Shaoshang)

graphite on watercolor paper
19x19(cm)

翔羽 (Sho-U)
ink on Kent paper
72.7x72.7(cm)

2 4

回回 (HuiHui)

graphite on watercolor paper
41x31.8(cm)

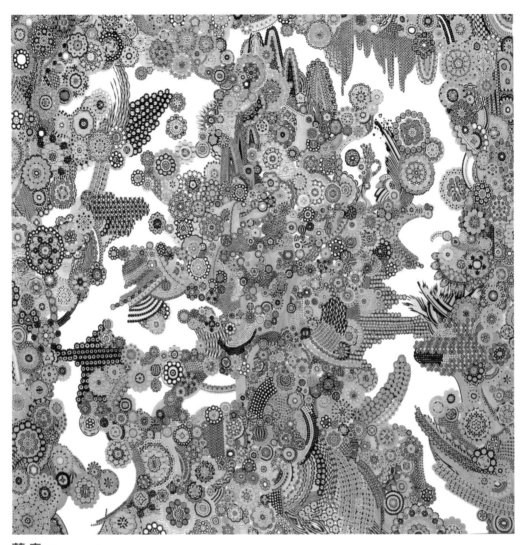

蓬 堯 (Hougyo)

ink on Kent paper
91x91(cm)

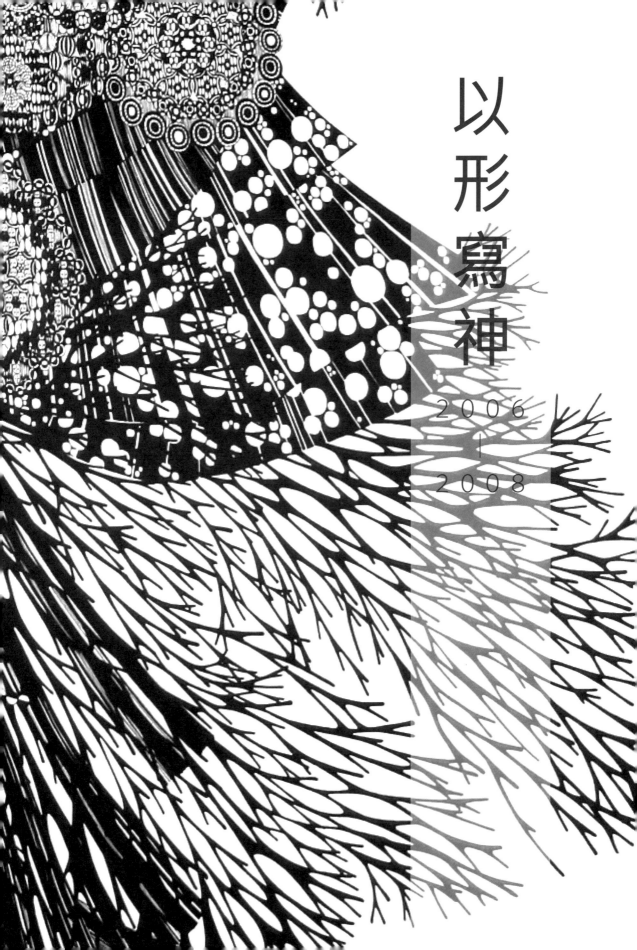

以形寫神

2006
|
2008

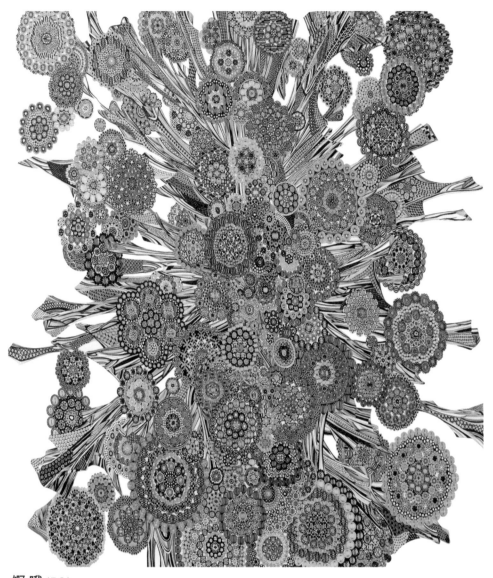

婀 哦 (EO)

ink on Kent paper
91x91(cm)

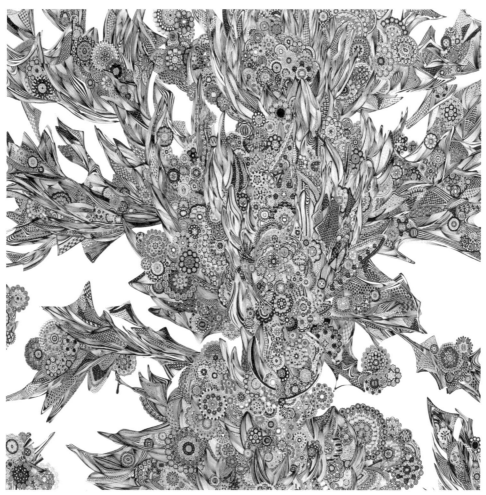

蝕蝕 (Shokushoku)

ink on Kent paper
91x91(cm)

壺臺 (RutsuBo)

ink on Kent paper
72.7x91(cm)

嘸 貌 (TongBo)
ink on Kent paper
91x116.7(cm)

沙玖 (Saku)
ink on Kent paper
116.7x91(cm)

梟禹 (Xiao-U)
ink on Kent paper
116.7x91(cm)

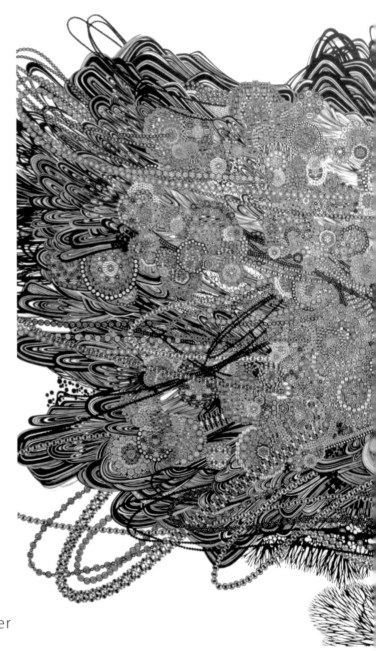

无哦无(W.O.W)
ink on Kent paper
112x162(cm)

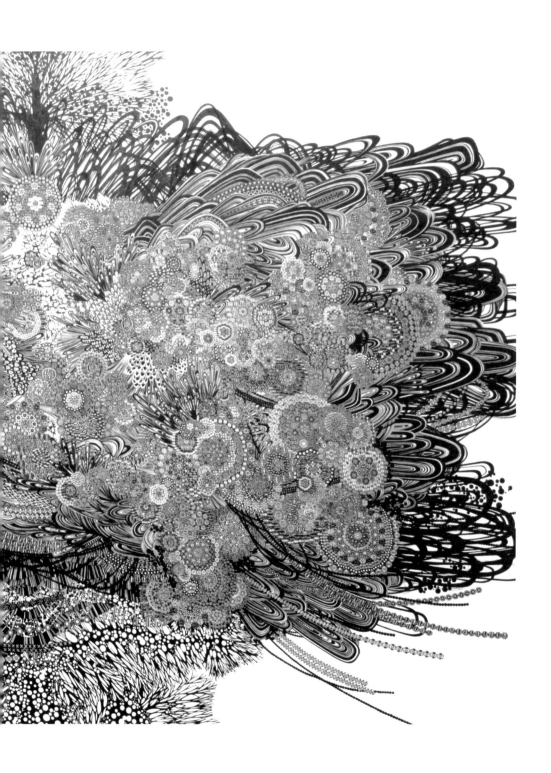

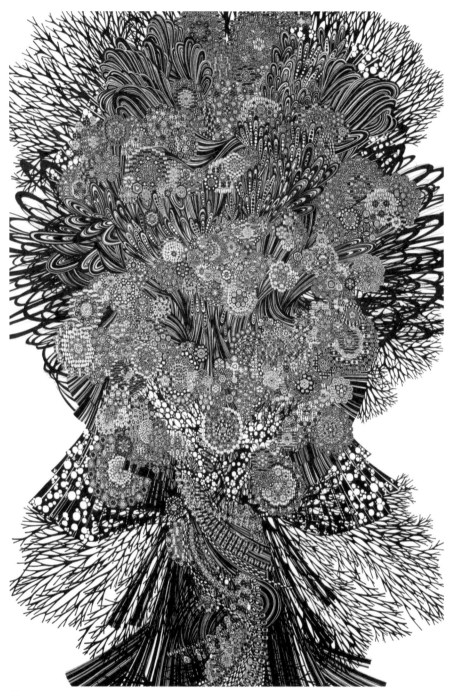

菩卯菩卯(BouBou)
ink on Kent paper
100x62.2(cm)

言彩

2010
—
2011

豸豸 (ZhiZhi)

ink on Kent paper
15.8x22.7(cm)

曄 (Ye)

ink on Kent paper
22.7x15.8 (cm)

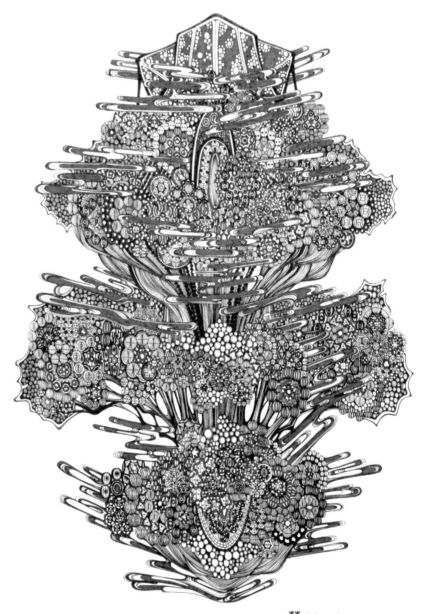

營 (Ying)

ink on Kent paper
22.7x15.8 (cm)

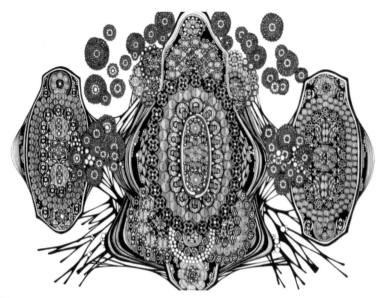

**噐** (Qi)

ink on Kent paper
15.8x22.7(cm)

**爰** (Yuan)

ink on Kent paper
15.8x22.7(cm)

丗(shi)

ink on Kent paper
15.8x22.7(cm)

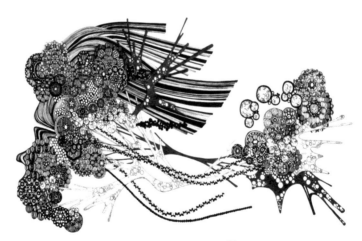

爬(pa)

ink on Kent paper
15.8x22.7(cm)

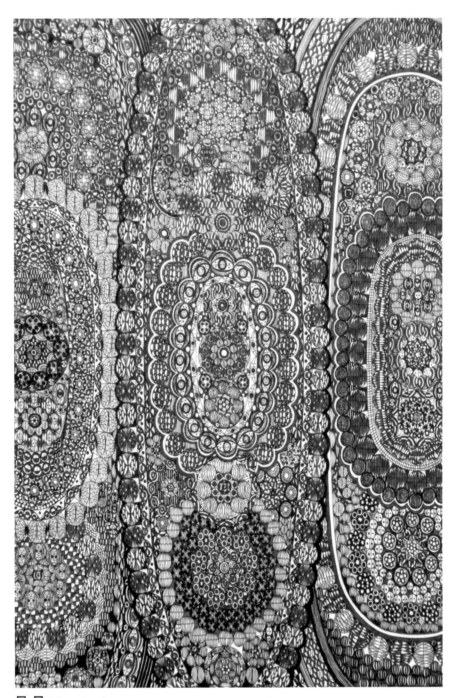

晶晶 (JingJing)

ink on Kent paper
22.7x15.8(cm)

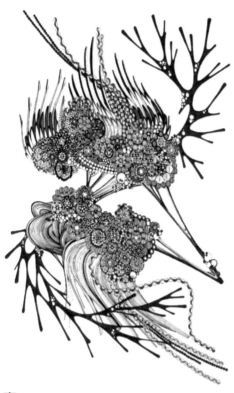

罋(Ji)
ink on Kent paper
22.7x15.8(cm)

瓮(Weng)
ink on Kent paper
22.7x15.8(cm)

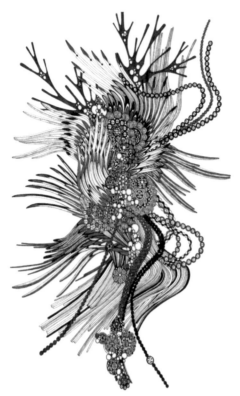

炙 (Zhi)
ink on Kent paper
22.7x15.8(cm)

ㅓ (Pan)
ink on Kent paper
22.7x15.8(cm)

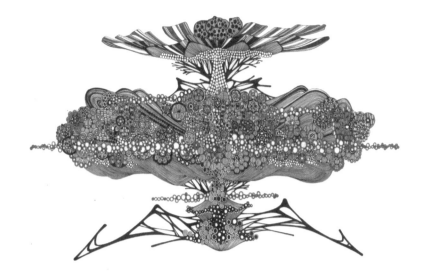

夲 (Tao)

ink on Kent paper
15.8x22.7(cm)

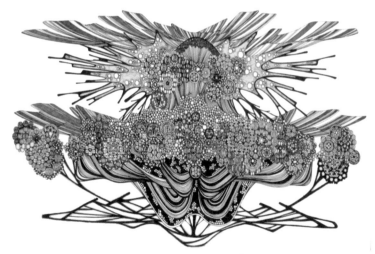

恚 (Hui)

ink on Kent paper
15.8x22.7(cm)

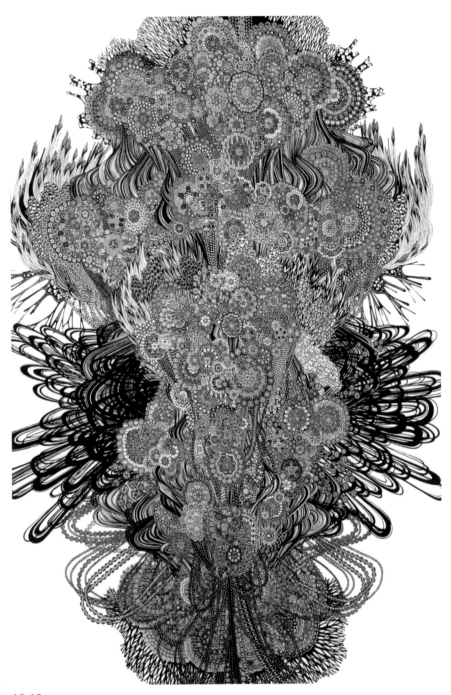

姚 姚 (YaoYao)
ink on Kent paper
130.3x60(cm)

咫咫 (ZhiZhi)
ink on Kent paper
72.7x60.6(cm)

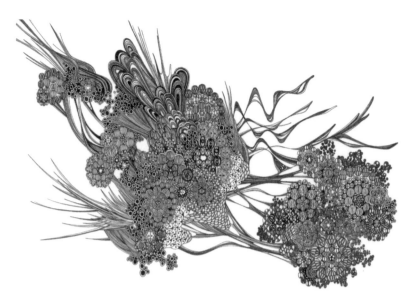

**氿** (Ya)

ink on Kent paper
15.8x22.7(cm)

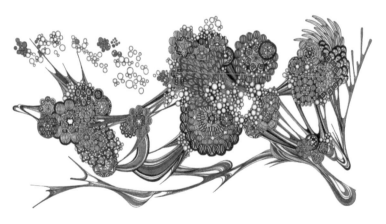

**夭** (Yao)

ink on Kent paper
15.8x22.7(cm)

蕭(Shan)

ink on Kent paper
15.8x22.7(cm)

庵(An)

ink on Kent paper
19x19(cm)

青奏青 (SeiSoSei)
ink on Kent paper
116.7x72.7(cm)

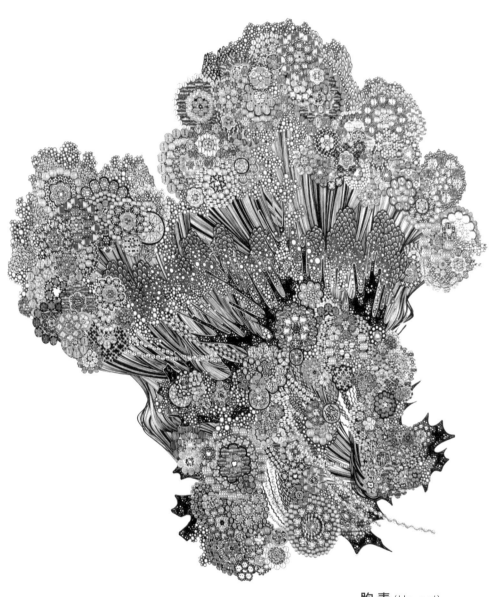

胞青 (Ho-sei)
ink on Kent paper
53x45.5(cm)

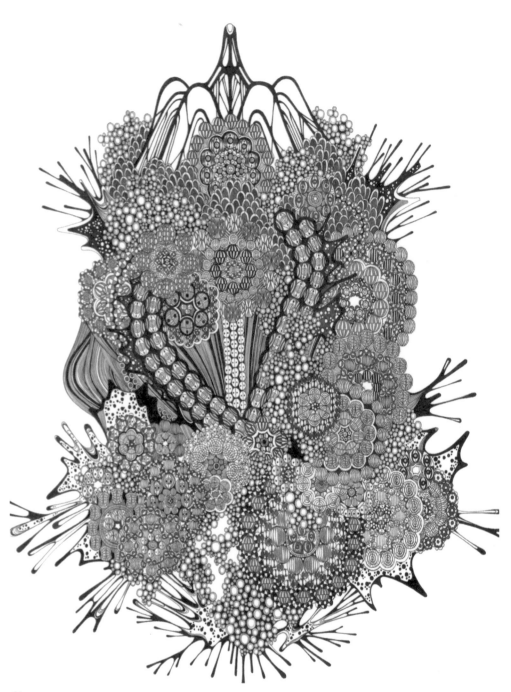

奠 (Ten)

ink on Kent paper
27.3x22(cm)

尭 (Gyo)

ink on Kent paper
19x14(cm)

畠 (Fu)

ink on Kent paper
22.7x15.8(cm)

蜃 (Shen)

ink on Kent paper
22.7x15.8(cm)

研細

2 0 1 2
|
2 0 1 4

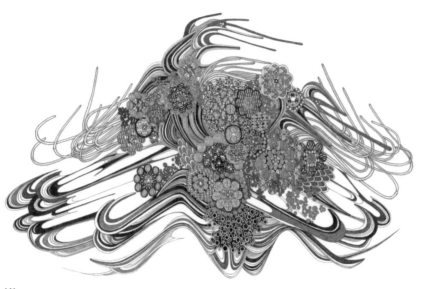

熾 (Bi)
ink on Kent paper
22x27.3(cm)

丩 (Jiu)
ink on Kent paper
22.7x15.8(cm)

夘 (Yo)
ink on Kent paper
15.8x22.7(cm)

鬲 (Li)

ink on Kent paper
22.7x15.8(cm)

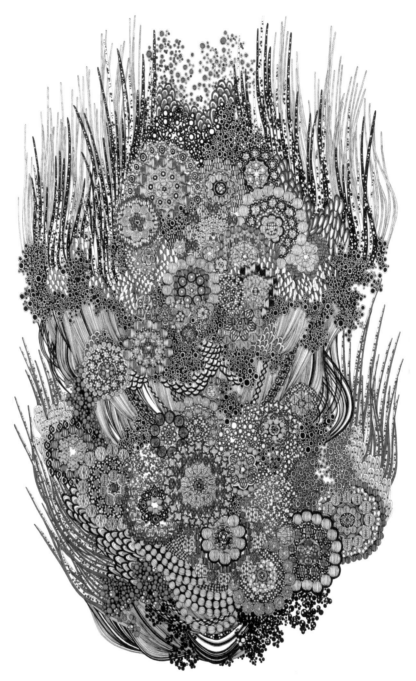

龠 (Yue)

ink on Kent paper
41x24.2(cm)

蠢 (Quan)

ink on Kent paper
41x24.2(cm)

朝藍青 (ChoRanSei)
ink on Kent paper
72.2x60.6(cm)

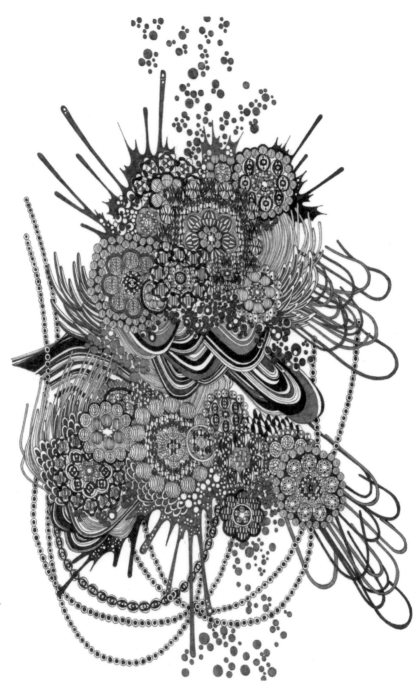

龜 (Gui)
ink on Kent paper
22.7x15.8(cm)

噩 (Ngok)

ink on Kent paper
33.4x53(cm)

夔 (Ki)

ink on Kent paper
22x33.3(cm)

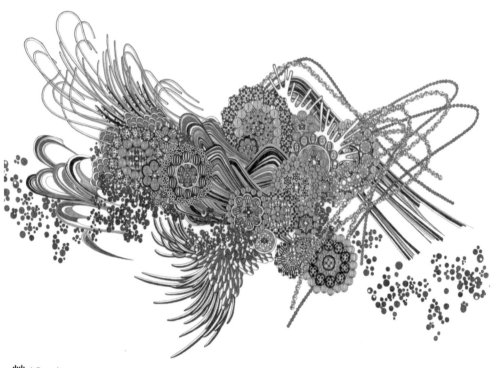

艸 (Cao)
ink on Kent paper
22.2x27.4(cm)

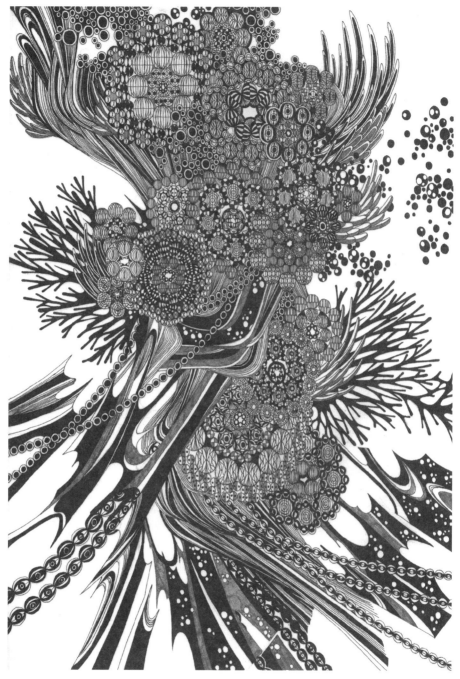

茲 (KoKo)

ink on Kent paper
22.7x15.8(cm)

渺 (Byo)
ink on Kent paper
33.3x22(cm)

渺渺 (ByoByo)
ink on Kent paper
116.7x72(cm)

蘦 (Tian)
ink on Kent paper
70x60.3(cm)

忎(Ren)

ink on Kent paper
15.8x22.7(cm)

籢(Lian)

ink on Kent paper
22.7x15.8(cm)

紅 (Hon)

ink on Kent paper
22.7x15.8(cm)

**靘** (Cheng)

ink on Kent paper
19x14(cm)

**桐** (Do)

ink on Kent paper
22.7x15.8(cm)

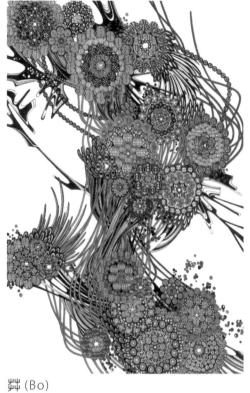

飆 (Biao)
ink on Kent paper
22.7x15.8(cm)

芔 (Bo)
ink on Kent paper
33.3x22(cm)

繾綣

2015
—
2018

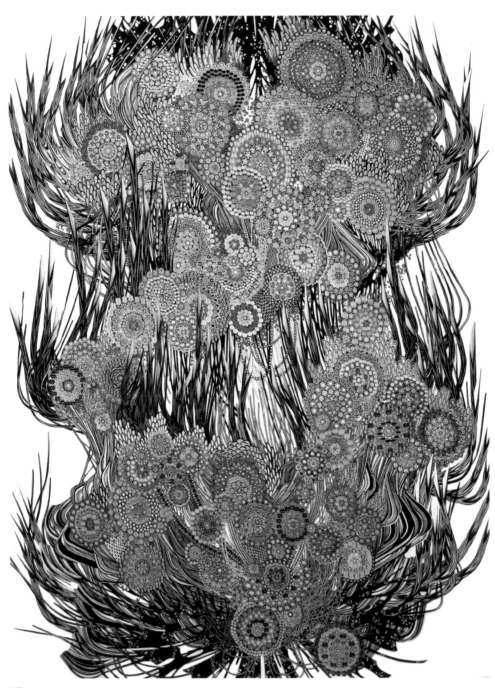

囑(Shok)
ink on Kent paper
116.7x91(cm)

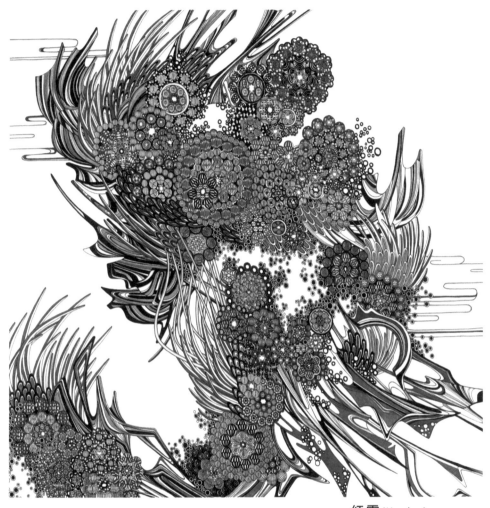

紅霄(Kosho)

ink on Kent paper
30x30(cm)

畚(HuGo)
ink on Kent paper
41x31.8(cm)

紅翅(Hongchi)

ink on Kent paper
22.7x15.8(cm)

粦(Lin)

ink on Kent paper
30x30(cm)

朱鳥(Akamitori)

ink on Kent paper
15.8x22.7(cm)

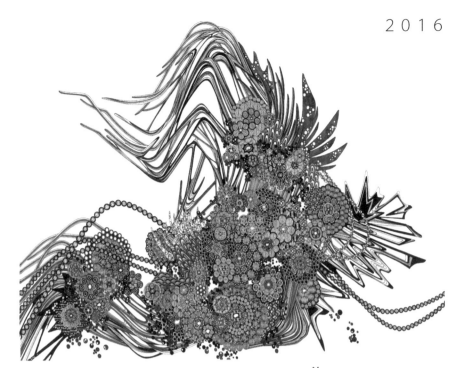

汐(Suisei)
ink on Kent paper
41x31.8(cm)

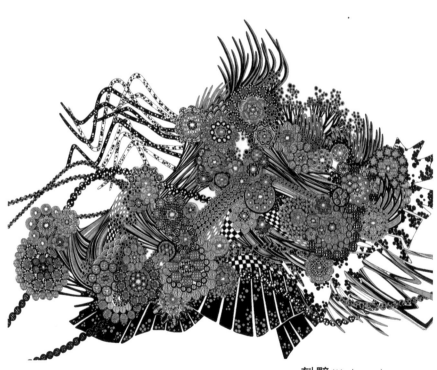

刻黯(Kokuan)
ink on Kent paper
31.8x41(cm)

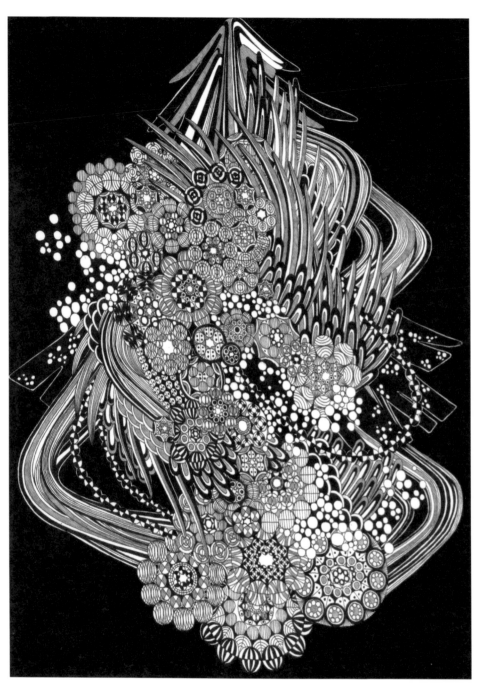

黯ノ一(Annoichi)

ink on Kent paper
22.7x15.8(cm)

瀧(Sei)
ink on Kent paper
30x30(cm)

紅妧(Koyuan)
ink on Kent paper
72.7x60.6(cm)

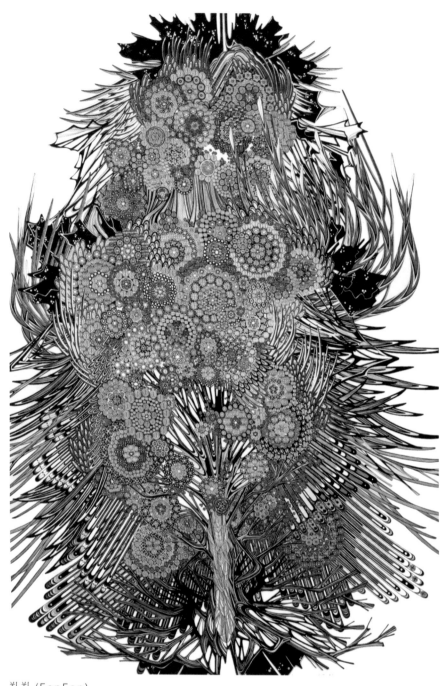

犾犾 (FenFen)

ink on Kent paper
91x60.6(cm)

紅尭(Kogyo)

ink on Kent paper
15.8x22.7(cm)

**漪**(Nami)

ink on Kent paper
41x31.8(cm)

刺紅(Shikou)

ink on Kent paper
41x31.8(cm)

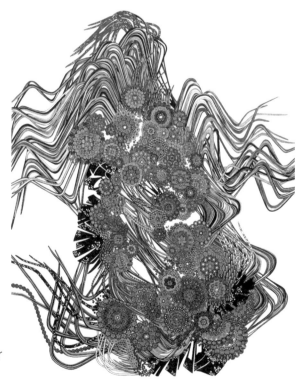

颭(Kai)

ink on Kent paper
70x60.3(cm)

嗥(Hao)

ink on Kent paper
22.7x15.8(cm)

彎(Wan)

ink on Kent paper
15.8x22.7(cm)

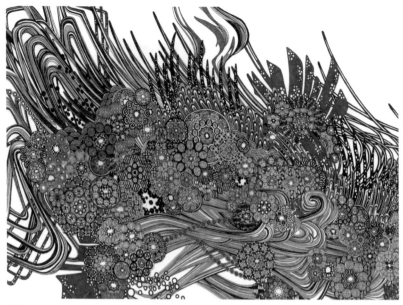

軌丰(Kibou)

ink on Kent paper
24.2x33.3(cm)

瓠(Hisago)

ink on Kent paper
24.2x33.3(cm)

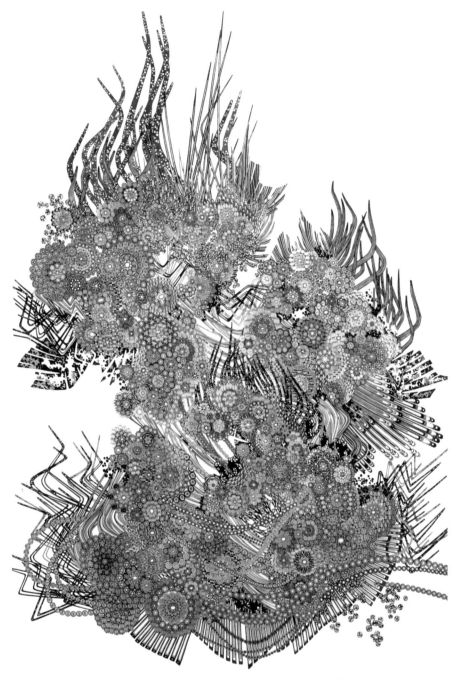

青盛(Seisei)
ink on Kent paper
116.7x80.3(cm)

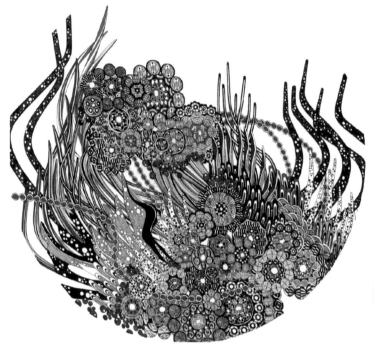

冂 (Jing)

ink on Kent paper
Φ22.7(cm)

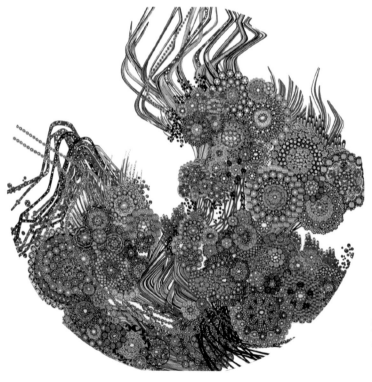

靚靚(SeiSei)

ink on Kent paper
Φ53(cm)

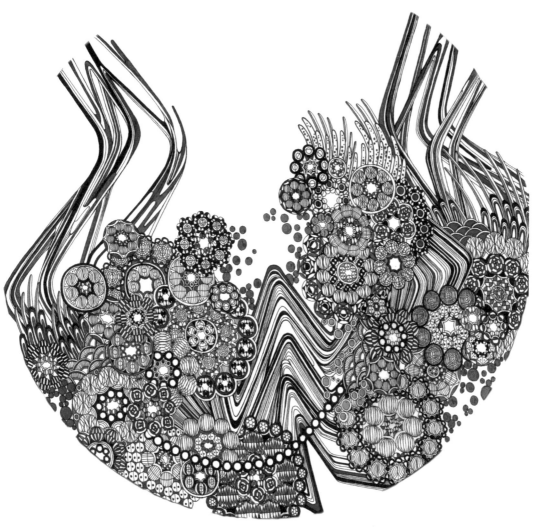

紅蔆(Koai)
ink on Kent paper
Φ22.7(cm)

冃 (Mao)
ink on Kent paper
Φ22.7(cm)

紫蓉(Shiyo)
ink on Kent paper
22.7x15.8(cm)

靉靆(Aikan)
ink on Kent paper
116.7x91(cm)

## List of works

- 厎Zha · graphite on watercolor paper · 15.8x22.7 cm · 2003年 · P.16
- 阿A · graphite on watercolor paper · 15.8x22.7 cm · 2003年 · P.16
- 眼之一 · graphite on watercolor paper · 53x45.5 cm · 2003年 · P.17
- 眼之二 · graphite on watercolor paper · 53x53 cm · 2003年 · P.17
- 眼之三 · graphite on watercolor paper · 53x53.1 cm · 2003年 · P.18
- 妝眼Shoyan · graphite on watercolor paper · 15.8x22.7 cm · 2003年 · P.19
- 茫Bou · graphite on watercolor paper · 2004年 · P.20
- 叕叕Tetsutetsu · graphite on watercolor paper · 72.7x72.7 cm · 2004年 · P.21
- 斑眼Madarame · graphite on watercolor paper · 53x53 cm · 2004年 · P.21
- 胎華TaiKa · graphite on watercolor paper · 41x31.8 cm · 2004年 · P.22
- 渾渾KonKon · graphite on watercolor paper · 38x45.5 cm · 2004年 · P.22
- 蠢蠢ShunShun · graphite on watercolor paper · 41x31.8 cm · 2004年 · P.23
- 小暘Shaoshang · graphite on watercolor paper · 19x19 cm · 2004年 · P.23
- 翔羽Sho-U · ink on Kent paper · 72.7x72.8 cm · 2005年 · P.24
- 回回HuiHui · graphite on watercolor paper · 41x31.8 cm · 2005年 · P.25
- 蓬堯Hougyo · ink on Kent paper · 91x91 cm · 2005年 · P.26
- 婀哦EO · ink on Kent paper · 91x91 cm · 2006年 · P.28
- 蝕蝕Shokushoku · ink on Kent paper · 91x91 cm · 2006年 · P.29
- 壺臺RutsuBo · ink on Kent paper · 72.7x91 cm · 2007年 · P.30
- 嗔貌TongBo · ink on Kent paper · 91x116.7 cm · 2007年 · P.31
- 沙玖Saku · ink on Kent paper · 116.7x91 cm · 2008年 · P.32
- 梟禹Xiao-U · ink on Kent paper · 116.7x91 cm · 2008年 · P.33
- 无哦无W.O.W · ink on Kent paper · 112.0x162 cm · 2009年 · P.34-35
- 菩卯菩卯BouBou · ink on Kent paper · 100x62.2 cm · 2008年 · P.36
- 豸豸zhizhi · ink on Kent paper · 15.8x22.7 cm · 2010年 · P.38
- 曄Ye · ink on Kent paper · 22.7x15.8 cm · 2010年 · P.38
- 營Ying · ink on Kent paper · 22.7x15.8 cm · 2010年 · P.39
- 罨Qi · ink on Kent paper · 15.8x22.7 cm · 2010年 · P.40
- 爰Yuan · ink on Kent paper · 15.8x22.7 cm · 2010年 · P.40
- 爬Pa · ink on Kent paper · 72.7x60.6 cm · 2010年 · P.41
- 丗shi · ink on Kent paper · 15.8x22.7 cm · 2010年 · P.41
- 晶晶JingJing · ink on Kent paper · 22.7x15.8 cm · 2010年 · P.42